Apollo and the Battle of the Birds

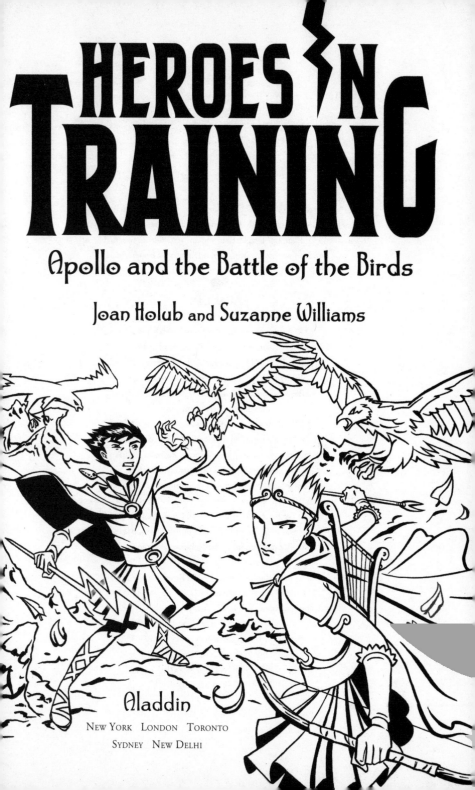

HEROES IN TRAINING

Apollo and the Battle of the Birds

Joan Holub and Suzanne Williams

Aladdin

NEW YORK   LONDON   TORONTO
SYDNEY   NEW DELHI

ALADDIN

An imprint of Simon & Schuster Children's Publishing Division
1230 Avenue of the Americas, New York, NY 10020
First Aladdin hardcover edition April 2014
Text copyright © 2014 by Joan Holub and Suzanne Williams
Illustrations copyright © 2014 by Craig Phillips
All rights reserved, including the right of reproduction
in whole or in part in any form.
ALADDIN is a trademark of Simon & Schuster, Inc.,
and related logo is a registered trademark of Simon & Schuster, Inc.
For information about special discounts for bulk purchases,
please contact Simon & Schuster Special Sales
at 1-866-506-1949 or business@simonandschuster.com.
The Simon & Schuster Speakers Bureau can bring authors to your live event.
For more information or to book an event,
contact the Simon & Schuster Speakers Bureau at 1-866-248-3049
or visit our website at www.simonspeakers.com.
Jacket designed by Karin Paprocki
Interior designed by Mike Rosamilia
The text of this book was set in Adobe Garamond Pro.
Manufactured in the United States of America 0715 FFG
2 4 6 8 10 9 7 5 3
Library of Congress Control Number 2014930550
ISBN 978-1-4424-8845-8 (pbk)
ISBN 978-1-4424-8846-5 (hc)
ISBN 978-1-4424-8847-2 (eBook)

⚡ Contents ⚡

Greetings, Mortal Readers,

I am Pythia, the Oracle of Delphi, in Greece. I have the power to see the future. Hear my prophecy:

Ahead I see donkeys lurking. Wait—make that *danger* lurking. (The future can be blurry, especially when my eyeglasses are foggy.)

Anyhoo, beware! Titan giants seek to rule all of Earth's domains—oceans, mountains, forests, and the depths of the Underwear. Oops— make that *Underworld*. Led by King Cronus, they are out to destroy us all!

Yet I foresee hope. A band of rightful rulers called Olympians will arise. Though their size and youth are no match for the Titans, they will be giant in heart, mind, and spirit. They await their leader—a very special boy. One who is destined to become king of the gods and ruler of the heavens.

If he is brave enough.

And if he and his friends work together as one. And if they can learn to use their new amazing tragic powers—um, *magic* powers—in time to save the world!

CHAPTER ONE

Strange Tracks

R eady, set, grow!"

Ten-year-old Demeter threw one magical glittering, oval-shaped yellow seed into the air. It landed in a field of brown dirt and withered weeds.

Suddenly the field began to glow and glimmer. Rows of golden wheat sprang up next to rows of green, leafy vegetables and trees bearing figs and apples.

Six other Olympians, who were all her same age, stood behind her and watched with wide eyes. They had seen Demeter do this before, but it was still amazing every time.

Blond, blue-eyed Apollo strummed on his lyre, singing:

"A field that once was brown and lean
Is now so healthy and so green!"

Hestia's brown eyes sparkled, and she clapped her hands together. "Demeter, it's beautiful!"

Demeter smiled, pleased, and blushed a little.

Behind them the residents of the small village began to clap and cheer. Young children ran into the field, staring at the plants in wonder.

The village elder, a small, gray-haired woman, approached the Olympian god's young leader,

Zeus. She grabbed his hands in her strong grip.

"Thank you," she said, her pale eyes glistening with tears of joy. "We have suffered greatly since that horrible Titan Hyperion burned our fields so we could not grow crops. But you have brought us rain and water, and now this. For the first time in many days, I feel hopeful that we will survive. You are our hero."

Zeus grinned. "Well, it wasn't just me. It was all of us working together." He nodded toward the other Olympians. "And now Demeter's Magic Seeds are growing new crops."

Poseidon stepped over to Zeus and slung an arm around his shoulders. He waved the long-handled, three-pronged golden trident he'd gotten when he'd discovered he was god of the sea. "And my boltbrain bro and I combined our powers to whip up a nice rainy storm to fill your wells. 'Zap! Bam! Sizzle!'"

"Who are you calling 'boltbrain,' Fishlips?" Zeus demanded with a grin.

Laughing, Poseidon lunged toward him with the trident, mock-fighting. Zeus held up Bolt, the magical lightning bolt he carried.

"Bolt, large!" Zeus commanded. Instantly it sprang from dagger-size to the size of Zeus. *Zing!* Zeus pretended to fend Poseidon off with it.

Hera stepped up to them, her blue eyes snapping with annoyance as she flipped her long blond hair back over her shoulder. "Those are magical objects, not toys," she scolded. Then she turned to Poseidon. "And since when do you call Zeus 'bro'?" she asked.

"Since I found out we were brothers, duh," Poseidon said, beginning to twirl his trident. "We're almost like twins."

Zeus and Poseidon did look alike, both with the same wavy hair, but Zeus's eyes were the color of the sky he commanded, and Poseidon's were turquoise, like the sea.

Humpf. "Well, you better not start calling me 'sis,'" Hera warned.

Just two weeks before, six of the Olympians—Zeus, Poseidon, Hera, Hades, Hestia, and Demeter—had learned that they all had the same mother. Her name was Rhea and they hadn't seen her since they were born. Zeus had been raised away from the others by a nymph, a goat, and a bee. And suddenly discovering he had brothers and sisters had been a delicious feeling.

"You can call me 'bro' all you want, Bro," Zeus told Poseidon.

The village elder spread her arms wide and spoke again. "We thank all of you! Please take anything you need for your journey from our fields. We have some bread and cheese we can give you too. Is there anything else you might need?"

Demeter looked down at her tunic, which was torn and stained after their recent encounter with a giant beanstalk. The other Olympians were looking pretty ragged too after weeks on the road.

"Um, do you guys have any spare clothes?" she asked.

The woman nodded. "Of course. I'm sure we can find something for each of you."

"Thanks," Zeus said. "I think we're all set, then. Clothes, food, and weapons."

Zeus shaded his eyes against the sun. In the distance a flock of birds slowly flew in a circle. When the sun hit them, they sparkled. Weird. He had been seeing them for days. Those sparkly birds had him a little worried.

At the word "weapons" some of the villagers came closer. "'Weapons'? Why would you need weapons?" asked one grizzled farmer.

"King Cronus doesn't exactly like the fact that

we're going around fixing what his giant Titan buddies are messing up around the Earth," Zeus replied. "His Crony soldiers are always after us, and then we usually end up running into monsters, and, well . . . we need weapons to fight them and protect ourselves. Some of us have magical objects that can be used in fights. But not all of us do."

Hera folded her arms across her chest and glared at Zeus when he said this. She was one of the Olympians without a magical object. Apollo didn't have one either, but he didn't seem to mind, the way she did. At the moment he was happily strumming his lyre, singing a tune while some of the village children danced.

The old man nodded. "King Cronus is no friend to anyone here. He and his henchmen Cronies are always stomping on our fields and stealing whatever they like from us. Not to mention trying to take over the world."

Hades stuck out one arm and pulled back his other, pretending to cock a bow and then shoot an arrow from it. "Not if we can help it! If we run into those Cronies, I can put on my helmet, turn invisible, and shoot at our enemies with my bow and arrows. They'll never know what hit them!"

"It's lucky we found those bows and arrows in that abandoned hunting cabin," Hera said, glaring at Zeus, "seeing as not *all* of us are lucky enough to have magical objects of our own! Now at least all of us have weapons, even if they aren't magical."

"Here is something you should know: I am excellent with a bow," Apollo said, using rhyme-speak, as he often did.

"I just hope we won't have to use them," Demeter added.

The villagers scattered to gather cheese and bread while the Olympians happily filled the packs they were given with fruit and vegetables from the field. Before long they were back on the road to the town of Corinth, dressed in new tunics and carrying packs of food.

"Hey," Poseidon complained, glancing at Apollo as they walked along, "how come I didn't get the blue tunic, instead of this orange one? I'm the ruler of the sea, after all. And blue is the color of the sea."

"It's true that you are ruler of the sea, but this blue tunic fits great on me," Apollo replied.

"Stop complaining and just be glad that we haven't seen a sign of the Cronies in days," Hades said to Poseidon.

"Maybe we've lost them," said Demeter.

"I wouldn't be so sure," Hera said darkly. "They always seem to turn up, no matter how hard we try to throw them off our trail."

"But we're in the middle of nowhere," Poseidon said, looking around. The path to Corinth was taking them across a wide, mountainous area. They tried to stick to the foothills, but there were steep climbs along the trail. "Why is Pythia sending us all the way to Lake Stymphalia to find a shield, anyway?"

"Stymphalia . . . ," Apollo repeated. "I swear I've heard of that somewhere before. Stymphalia . . . Stymphalia . . ."

"It's not just any shield. It's an aegis," Zeus reminded Poseidon, pronouncing it "EE-jiss." "It must be super-special, or she wouldn't make us go to all this trouble to find it."

"It had better be," Apollo said, his usually bright eyes growing dark. "I really wanted to go off on my own to find my twin sister, Artemis, but I promised Pythia we'd all stick together."

Pythia, the Oracle of Delphi, had been sending the Olympians on quests ever since they'd gotten together. The guests had three goals: to find more Olympians; to gather magical objects; and finally, to defeat the evil King Cronus. When they last saw Pythia, she told them to win the aegis through battle.

"Hera, are we still on course?" Zeus asked.

Hera looked at the stone amulet that hung around her neck. It was named Chip and belonged to Zeus. He'd gotten it in Delphi when he'd found Bolt, his magical object. He felt bad that Hera didn't have her own object yet, so he let her wear Chip, an oval-shaped smooth, gray stone.

Chip was very useful. It could talk when it wanted to, in its own language (Chip Latin). Also, if you asked it a question, writing would appear to give you the answer. It even showed them maps sometimes.

"Which way to Lake Stymphalia, Chip?" Hera asked. Instantly a glowing arrow appeared on the surface of the stone, pointing straight ahead. She grinned. "Looks like we're good."

"If you call being hungry and tired and stuck in an orange tunic 'good,' then yes, we're good," Poseidon grumbled.

They walked on for a while longer, crossing a desertlike plain with mountains rising all around. But as they got closer to Corinth, the land was greener, with thick forest all surrounding them. The ground under their feet was damp and muddy.

Suddenly Hera stopped walking. "That's a strange track," she said, kneeling to stare at the ground. "It looks like a human foot. But there's only one. See? And there's another track a few feet ahead."

"A few feet? I thought you said it was one foot," Poseidon joked.

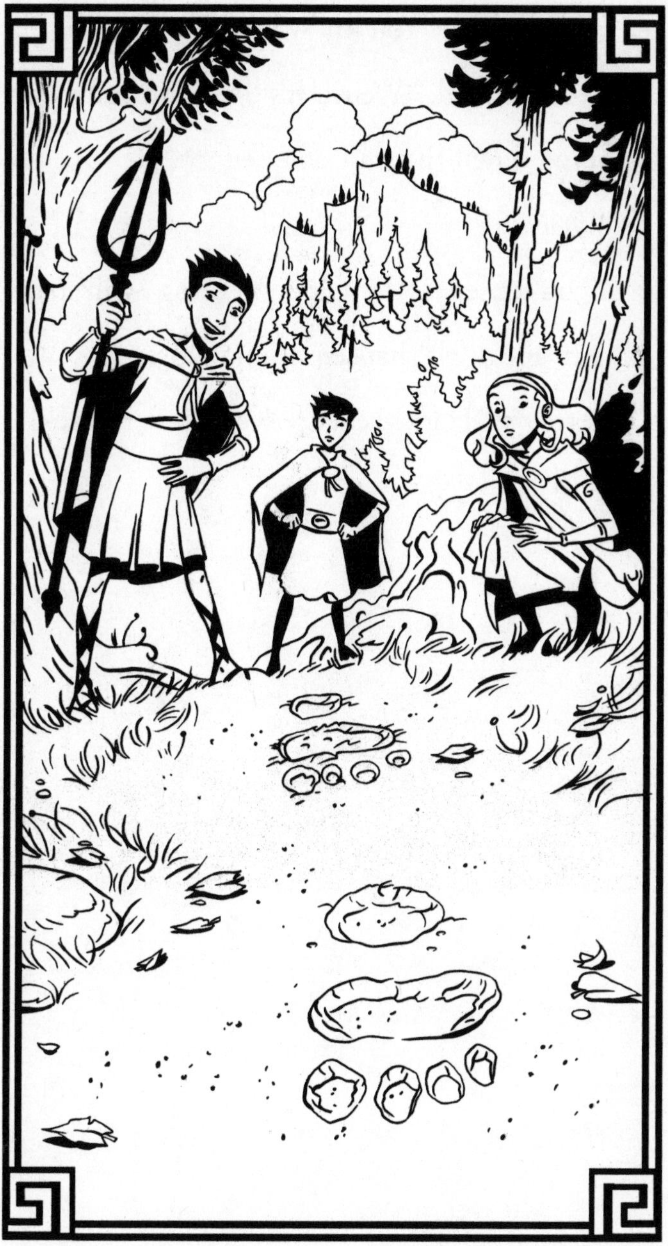

Hera sighed. "You know what I meant!"

Zeus nodded. "Weird. It's like somebody was hopping down the trail on one foot."

Whooosh!

Zeus tensed as he felt something whiz past his ear. He'd felt that sensation before.

"Arrows!" Hades yelled. "We're under attack!"

CHAPTER TWO

Attack of the Sciapods

Zeus whipped around and saw a small army of men hopping down the trail behind them. They were hopping because, although they looked like normal men from the waist up, each had just one big, thick leg where there were usually two. And one very large foot!

"What are they?" Hestia asked, her eyes wide.

Apollo burst into song.

"These monsters are the Sciapods,

And it is true, they do look odd.

Each Sciapod has just one foot.

But it doesn't mean they will stay put.

They'll hop until they chase you down,

and shoot their arrows at your crown."

Hades quickly put on his magical object—a Helm of Darkness—and turned invisible. "If by 'crown' you mean 'head,' then I'll protect mine with this," he said.

"Hades, use your bow!" Zeus commanded, immediately falling into battle mode. "Everyone else, take cover. Behind that boulder over there!"

Hades's arrows kept the charging Sciapods at bay until the other Olympians reached the rock. There Zeus pulled Bolt from the sheath at his waist.

"Bolt, large!" he commanded. A sound like

ice cracking on a frozen pond filled the air as the lightning-bolt-shaped dagger grew to be as large as Zeus. It crackled with electricity.

Zeus barked out more orders. "Poseidon, see if you can blast those One-Footers with a water wave! Hestia, do what you can to get these guys to hotfoot it out of here."

"Hotfoot?" Hestia asked, confused at first. But then she glanced down at the magic torch she held. "Right. Got it!" she said.

The Sciapods were just a few yards away now, and they were even scarier-looking up close than they had been from a distance. Their curly hair was tangled, their grins were nasty, and their eyes blazed with fury. Each of them wore a simple loincloth.

"What are we waiting for?" Hera yelled from behind Zeus. Then she scooped up a handful of rocks and began pelting them at the Sciapods.

 17

She nailed one right in the forehead, and the monster fell down, before struggling to get back up on his foot.

"Looks like we're getting off on the wrong foot with these guys!" quipped Hades.

"Less jokes, more arrows!" Hera scolded him.

"You have a bow too!" Hades shot back.

Hera tossed more rocks, taking down yet another Sciapod. "Yeah, but I think my rock-throwing arm is pretty good."

Apollo and Demeter picked up their bows and also started shooting. But it was hard to aim, with the Sciapods jumping up and down.

At the same time Zeus, Poseidon, and Hestia launched their attacks.

Poseidon pointed his trident at a Sciapod hurtling toward him. *Sploosh!* He blasted the creature back with a strong jet of water.

Hestia held up her torch, concentrating. A small fireball exploded near one of the Sciapod's toes. He let out a yelp and began to jump up and down, dropping his bow.

"How's that for a hotfoot?" Hestia asked Zeus with a grin.

Zeus smiled back at her. She'd obviously learned a little something from their last quest against the Titan Hyperion and his fireballs! Quickly Zeus pointed his thunderbolt at an approaching Sciapod. A jolt of electricity burst from Bolt and zapped the Sciapod in the foot. The creature hopped up and down, shrieking. Then it fell to the ground, sticking its smoking toes into its mouth to cool them down.

"That guy's really put his foot in his mouth this time!" Hades joked.

Then . . . *Bam!* Following the sound of

Hades's voice, one of the Sciapods launched itself in the air and slammed his foot right into Hades's invisible chest. The young lord of the Underworld—a deep, dark realm beneath the Earth—tumbled backward. His Helm of Darkness fell off. He was visible again!

Thinking quickly, Zeus zapped the attacker with Bolt, which sent the Sciapod flying. Hades sat up, dazed and grateful.

"That one really put his best—*and only*—foot forward," he joked.

Zeus scanned the scene. By now every Sciapod was either knocked out cold or nursing a burned foot.

"Looks like we got 'em," he said.

Then he heard a voice behind him. The voice of the magic chip of the stone amulet Hera wore.

"Ore-mip oming-cip." When the stone spoke in Chip Latin, it moved the first letter of each word to the end of that word, and then added "ip."

"Chip says there are more coming!" Hera translated.

"I think I see them," Demeter reported, shading her eyes against the sun.

Zeus thought about their next move. They could stay and fight, but they were running out of arrows. Also, sometimes the power of his thunderbolt and the other magical objects ran out if they used them too much. Besides, who knew how many more Sciapods might come? There could be hundreds heading toward the Olympians.

"We should get out of here while we can," Zeus said. He nodded toward the dark forest to their right. "Maybe we can lose them in there."

"Let's move," Hera agreed. She broke into a run, and the others quickly followed.

CHAPTER THREE

In the Deep, Dark Forest

The Olympians raced into the forest. They didn't get far before the sun's light was swallowed up by the leafy branches overhead. The trees grew close together and were thick with leaves and crawling vines. It was almost like night had suddenly fallen.

Poseidon shivered. "Does this place give anyone else the creeps?" he asked.

"It feels homey to me," said Hades. In the

Underworld, where he ruled, everything was dark and gloomy.

Hestia held up her torch, and a soft glow lit up the faces of the seven Olympians. "I'll light the way," she said.

As they walked along, Hera said, "What was up with those things that attacked us, anyway?"

Apollo started to sing, "Those monsters were the Sciapods—"

"I get that," Hera interrupted him. "They were weird one-footed monsters who shot arrows at us. Do you think King Cronus sent them?"

Zeus nodded as he held back a low-hanging branch so the others could pass. "I think they were Creatures of Chaos," he said.

King Cronus had an army of different monsters that he kept sending out to destroy the Olympians. Luckily, none of them had succeeded—yet.

Hestia glanced over her shoulder at Zeus and

frowned. "I was hoping he and his armies had lost our trail. That's what it seemed like, anyway."

"Well, I'm thinking that our trail is pretty easy to follow," Zeus replied. "I mean, everywhere we go orchards and plants spring up."

Poseidon gave a snort. "Definitely easier to follow than a trail of breadcrumbs."

"Pythia told me to drop a seed in every village we came to," Demeter said, sounding hurt. "I'm just doing what she said. Using my Magic Seeds to help people."

"It's the right thing to do," Hestia said from beside her. "And you should keep doing it."

Hera was behind them. "I don't know," she said doubtfully. "Maybe you could hold off dropping seeds until we reach Lake Stymphalia, Demeter. We don't need any more monsters attacking us right now."

"Aw, you're just jealous because Demeter's

got the Magic Seeds and you don't," Poseidon needled her.

His words caused silence to fall over the rest of the Olympians. The gloomy forest air got even chillier. Everybody knew that Hera was upset about not having a magical object of her own, but until now nobody had dared to say it out loud. They all knew how angry she could get. All of them except Zeus and Apollo had lived with her in the smelly belly of the giant Titan King Cronus for years. But Poseidon couldn't resist teasing his sister.

"I'm *not* jealous of a bunch of seeds," Hera said firmly, her voice as cold as ice.

"Maybe the aegis will turn out to be your magical object," Hestia said hopefully. "You could wear it over your tunic."

Hera made a face. "I don't know. A shield doesn't sound all that exciting to me."

"It sounded pretty cool the way Pythia described it," Zeus offered. "It has one hundred tassels of pure gold hanging from it."

Hera gave him a small smile. "Oh yeah. I forgot about that."

Zeus was relieved. If we could keep Hera happy, everybody else would be happy too.

"We should pick up our pace," he said. He held up his thunderbolt, which had shrunk to the size of his arm. It glowed with a shimmering white light. "Bolt and Hestia's torch will light our path."

"Don't forget Chip," Hera said, holding the stone in her palm. A glowing arrow appeared, showing them the way to go and lending even a little more light to the darkness.

The Olympians continued on in the direction of Chip's arrow. Darkness surrounded them like a black fog. It was quiet, but not a pleasant quiet, unfortunately—more like an eerie, thick quiet that didn't feel natural.

And though Chip, Bolt, and the torch did help fight the darkness, it was becoming harder and harder to see. Even so, Zeus could make out Hera in front of him and Hestia and Hades by his side, but the light cast by the objects wasn't strong enough to illuminate the whole group.

Apollo, who was in the rear, softly sang a song.

> *"Into the woods the heroes go.*
> *Our hearts are brave but our spirits are low.*
> *The darkness is as black as tar,*
> *And we haven't traveled very far—"*

"What a depressing song," Hera interrupted. "Can you lay off the lyre for now?"

Apollo sighed. "Just trying to cheer everyone up."

"Are you still feeling comfy in this gloomy place?" Poseidon asked Hades.

"Not exactly," his brother said. "In the Underworld it's creepy, but it's also . . . peaceful, I guess. But this creepy is something else. It's . . ."

"Evil," Hera said, her voice flat. "I feel like I'm swimming in evil soup."

Zeus glanced up, hoping to see a break in the trees. Instead he saw something move in the tree branches. He stopped cold.

"Look," he said, holding Bolt up toward the trees. "Do you see something moving up there?"

"Nuh-uh," said Hestia.

The others didn't see it either. But as Bolt's shimmering light shone on the treetops, Zeus could have sworn he saw movement again.

"It's probably just the wind," Demeter said, but her voice sounded a little shaky and she and Hestia huddled more closely together.

As the others continued on, Zeus stayed put for a moment, staring overhead. In the black canopy above he thought he could make out little dots . . . tiny, red, glowing dots. Or were those . . . *eyes*?

"Look up," Zeus called out. The rest of the Olympians stopped and gazed upward. "They look like little red eyes!"

"Probably just bugs," Poseidon guessed, but his voice was as shaky as Demeter's had been.

"What kinds of bugs have red eyes?" Hera scoffed.

"Well, flies do, but they don't really glow," answered Hades. "Maybe it's some kind of glow-worm?"

Zeus shook his head. "Up that high? I don't know."

"Well, whatever they are, the sooner we get out of here, the sooner we'll get away from them," Hera pointed out. She consulted Chip's arrow. "Forward!" she called.

They kept walking into the gloom. Zeus strained to see farther in front of them, hoping for an end to the trees. But all around him there was a wall of darkness. Then out of nowhere came a mighty yell.

RAWR! A shadowy figure leaped out of the darkness ahead and charged toward the Olympians.

CHAPTER FOUR

Feathered Fiends

The Olympians screamed in terror. The flame on Hestia's torch tripled in size, feeding off her panic. The bright glow lit up their attacker.

It was Poseidon! He must have gone ahead and then doubled back on them. "Ha! Gotcha!" he cried, and then he doubled over laughing.

Hera tried to punch him in the arm, but he

managed to dodge her. "What is *wrong* with you?" she yelled.

"I was just kidding around," Poseidon said, still grinning. "You know, you've been grumpier than usual."

Hera shrugged. "Now that I know you're my brother, it sort of feels natural."

"Yeah, well, we've got armies of monsters and Titans and Cronies to fight," Zeus reminded them. "So we have to stop fighting with one another!"

"And scaring one another too," added Hestia, whose face was pale in the torchlight.

"All right, all right," Poseidon said. "I see your point. Let's get moving again."

They plodded on through the dark forest. The dead quiet they had felt earlier was replaced by strange sounds, like the rustling of branches and swooshes of wind, but they couldn't feel any breeze on their skin.

 35

"What was that?" Hades suddenly cried out.

"What was what?" Zeus asked.

"I felt something . . . whoosh behind me," Hades said.

"I felt it too," added Apollo. "But when I looked back, I didn't see anything."

"I think our imaginations are playing tricks on us," Hera said. She looked at the amulet she wore. "Come on, Chip, get us out of here! Where to next?"

"Isn't that, like, the five-hundredth time you've asked Chip for directions?" Poseidon asked.

"If it weren't for Chip, we'd be lost in this place," Hera reminded him.

"Lead the way, Hera," Zeus said.

They marched on in silence. Then, just when Zeus thought he couldn't take another second of the creepy darkness, he saw a weak sliver of light through the trees up ahead.

He pointed. "I think we're getting to the edge of the forest."

Demeter nodded. "Even the ground feels different." She pressed down with her foot on the path in front of her. "It's all . . . squishy."

"And smelly, too," said Hera, wrinkling her nose.

Hades sniffed the air. "Smells pretty good to me." Which made Hera let out a snort.

Zeus broke into a run, eager to be rid of the forest for good. Where the trees ended, a damp marsh began. Even though the canopy of treetops was gone, the sun still shone only weakly on the marsh. And the air still felt thick with gloom. Swamp plants with shiny green leaves, and skinny strands of marsh grass, poked up from the mud beneath his feet. Just past the marsh the pale sunlight illuminated a wide, black lake.

"I think we're here!" he cried. "Lake Stymphalia!"

Hera held up the amulet. "What do you say, Chip?" she asked it.

"Es-yip, ere-hip," the magic stone confirmed.

Zeus took a step into the marsh, and his foot immediately sunk into the sticky mud. "Gross!" he said. "But at least we're out of that—"

A thundering sound interrupted him. Zeus looked up to see an enormous black cloud rise from the roof of the forest behind them. Hideous shrieks filled the air as the cloud descended on the marsh.

"Jumping jellyfish!" Poseidon yelled. "That cloud is made up of birds!"

Poseidon was right. And there were thousands of them! Maybe even zillions. They cackled and cawed at the Olympians, and the sound was deafening.

For a moment the Olympians were too stunned and frightened to move. As the attacking flock of birds circled closer, Zeus got a better look at them. Each had a pair of evil, glowing red eyes. Their feathers appeared sharp and silver, like they were made of metal. And their fierce, heavy-looking claws shone like brass.

Instinct kicked in, and the Olympians ran in all directions, trying to get away. Zeus was heading for the lake when he remembered something.

You're supposed to lead these guys! he scolded himself. *You need a plan!*

He scanned the marsh. There was no way to defend themselves in this open ground. But they had been safe enough before, in the forest.

"Back into the woods!" he yelled to the others.

Screeeeech! The birds shrieked and swooped down from the sky, rocketing at the Olympians like missiles.

Hestia had heeded his suggestion and was already at the forest's edge, with Apollo at her heels. Poseidon ran in from Zeus's left, and Hera and Demeter charged up on Zeus's right.

"These are some angry birds, Bro!" Poseidon yelled as he sprinted past.

Then Demeter let out a cry. From the corner of his eye, Zeus saw her trip and fall facedown into the marsh. Hera quickly reached to help her up, but Demeter gave a yelp.

"I hurt my ankle," she said, tears filling her eyes as she set up.

Zeus raced over to his sisters. He and Hera each grabbed one of Demeter's arms. Together, they picked her up and carried her back into the forest.

"Hey! Wait for me, guys!"

It was Hades, plodding toward them through the middle of the marsh. Zeus watched in horror as the birds dove right at Hades.

Whirring sounds filled the air as the birds began to shoot feathers that were sharp as arrows. Hades froze in his tracks.

"Heeeeeeeelp!" he yelled, sounding terrified.

Suddenly mounds of white glop dropped from the sky all around him. Where the glop hit the marsh grass, the plants instantly sizzled and died.

"It's deadly bird poop!" Poseidon shouted in horror.

Hades's brown eyes grew wide, but he was still too afraid to move.

"Hades, run!" Zeus commanded.

"Put on your helm!" added Hestia.

Remembering the helm seemed to unfreeze Hades. He quickly put it on and turned invisible.

The birds shrieked even louder now, angry and confused. More sharp feathers rained down from the sky as they circled over the spot where Hades had been.

Zeus held his breath, worried for his brother.

Would Hades make it safely back into the forest?

CHAPTER FIVE

It's Battle Time!

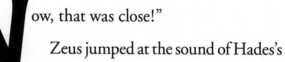ow, that was close!"

Zeus jumped at the sound of Hades's voice in his ear. Then Hades appeared before him, holding his helmet.

Hestia ran up and hugged him. "I'm so glad you're okay!"

Apollo snapped his fingers. "That's it!" he cried.

"That's what?" asked Hera.

"What I couldn't remember before," he said.

"Lake Stymphalia is special because of the Stymphalian *birds*!"

"'Special'?" asked Demeter. She was leaning against a tree, with her hurt left ankle extended in front of her. "I could think of a better word. Like maybe 'cursed'?"

"Cursed is right," agreed Hera. "So what do we do, oh mighty leader?" Her piercing blue eyes peered right at Zeus.

Before he could answer, Poseidon piped up instead. "I know what we should do. We should retrace our steps and get far away from those killer canaries!"

"We can't retreat," Zeus argued. "We have to go to Lake Stymphalia to get the aegis."

He gazed out past the edge of the trees toward the marsh. The birds circled the lake now, waiting. Suddenly they broke away from one another, darting in different directions across the sky. In seconds, hundreds of birds moved into formation, spelling out a word in the air: "CHICKENS."

"Will you look at that? They're not only dangerous; they're insulting!" Poseidon cried. "We've got to get out of here, I tell you!"

"But what about Demeter? She's hurt," Hestia pointed out.

Demeter gingerly put her foot down. "I'm okay. See?" she said bravely, but she winced when she tried to take a step.

"I hate to say it, but I think Boltbrain is right," said Hera, using one of her favorite nicknames for Zeus. "We've never backed down from a quest before."

"Exactly!" Zeus exclaimed. "Pythia said we'd have to do battle to get the aegis. So maybe she meant we'd have to battle these birds. They might have it stashed in a nest or something."

Poseidon shook his head. "How can we fight them all? Maybe Pythia can give us another quest instead." He cupped his hands around his mouth. "Pythia? Pythia? You there?" But the oracle did not appear.

"She doesn't come when you call her," Hera pointed out. "She just shows up when she wants to."

Apollo strummed on his lyre and began a new song.

"Down from the sky the weird birds did swoop.
Then they bombed us all with their poisonous poop.
As we once-brave heroes turned quickly and fled,
Some poop almost landed atop Hades's head."

"Hey!" Hades protested, sounding a little embarrassed. "That poop is deadly stuff! Did you see what it did to those plants? I'm not ready to live in the Underworld permanently, you know. And I bet none of the rest of you are either."

Apollo put down his lyre and shrugged. "Still, if we retreat now, that is the song that will be sung about our quest."

The seven Olympians looked at one another. They knew what Apollo meant. Nobody wanted to go down in history as a coward—Poseidon included.

"All right. Let's stay and fight," Poseidon said reluctantly. "But it won't be easy. There's a lot of them, and once we leave this forest, we won't have any cover. They'll poop all over us."

"Not if we take them down first," Zeus said. He nodded to the others. "We'll need to combine our magical objects this time, to increase our power."

"Do you think Demeter could use one of her seeds to make, like, a mega-weapon or something?" Hera asked. "Or a giant bird net?"

Demeter shook her head. "Oh no. I don't have that many seeds left, and I'd rather use them to save villages than to fight birds."

"But I can add my helmet to our magical power-up, right?" Hades asked.

"I have another idea for using the helmet," Zeus said. He knelt down, picked up a stick, and used it to draw a plan on the dirt path. The others watched and listened, nodding silently. For once they were in agreement.

When Zeus was done, he stood up. "All right, everybody," he said. "It's battle time!"

He, Poseidon, and Hestia stepped out of the forest onto the marsh. Immediately the circling birds turned in midair and started to fly toward them.

Hades put on his Helm of Darkness and followed behind the first three Olympians.

 49

"Here I go!" he called as he went invisible.

When the birds got closer, Zeus held out his thunderbolt. "Large," he commanded. As Bolt grew to its full size, Poseidon held up his trident, and Hestia held up her flaming torch.

"Let's do it!" Zeus yelled. The three Olympians touched their magical objects together. The weapons began to glow brightly with enormous power, sizzling with energy.

Boom! A bright, white light exploded from the top of the objects and cast a glow across the marsh. Frightened and confused, the birds broke formation for a few seconds.

"Olympians, attack!" Zeus shouted.

At Zeus's signal, Apollo, Hera, and Demeter—still limping—came out of the forest and took their positions. The seven Olympians created a C-formation around the edge of the marsh—Apollo farthest left, then Hera, Zeus, Poseidon,

Hestia, Demeter, and finally Hades, who stood closest to the birds yet was invisible to them.

Zeus thrust a fist into the air, and Hades immediately began to shoot arrows upward. Demeter joined in too.

Squawk! Squawk! Their arrows made contact! They knocked the birds off course—but couldn't penetrate their metal bodies.

"Maybe *these* arrows will do the trick," Hestia said, raising her supercharged torch. Its flames took the form of fiery arrows that zipped through the air. The first arrow hit a bird, exploding into a fireball and sending the bird spiraling into the water. *Ka-pow!*

"It worked!" Hestia cried happily as more mechanical birds exploded and began to rain down as bits of metal.

Sploosh! Next to her Poseidon was using his powered-up trident to shoot strong water blasts

at the birds. Just one blast knocked at least a dozen birds at a time out of the sky.

"Now, Bolt. Zap!" Zeus yelled. Immediately a jagged yellow charge of electricity launched into the air. It hit one metal bird and fried it, and then bounced off and hit another. Electricity loves metal, and Bolt's charge bounced from bird to bird, taking down one after another.

Farther down the edge of the marsh, Hera had abandoned her bow and was hurling rocks at a bird hovering over her head.

Whomp! A rock made contact and sent the bird reeling away.

Hera glanced over at Apollo, who was shooting arrow after arrow at the winged creatures with amazing speed. To her surprise the birds were falling as fast as the arrows hit them.

"How are you doing that?" she called out.

"Hades's and Demeter's arrows are bouncing off the metal!"

"They've got a weak spot right in the center of their foreheads," Apollo told the others. He drew an arrow in his bow and sent it flying. The arrow lodged in the bird's forehead, and the bird dropped from the sky. "Bull's-eye. Or rather, *bird's-eye*. See?"

Hera shook her head. "I don't get it. How come you couldn't take down those one-footed metal guys like this?"

"I didn't figure out their weak spot," Apollo replied. "I got lucky this time."

Suddenly the birds let out loud shrieks and began to dive straight at Demeter. Zeus pointed Bolt at the attackers and took out a line of them, but another line formed just behind the last.

"Demeter, catch!" Hades called out. Suddenly he appeared on the edge of the marsh, and

Demeter was holding his Helm of Darkness. She was startled for a second, but then she recovered and quickly put on the helmet.

The confused birds flew away from Demeter— and zoomed down behind Poseidon. They gripped his orange tunic with their sharp talons and began to lift him off the ground.

"Hey! Let go!" he yelled.

Zeus immediately pointed Bolt toward the birds, but then he heard Hera behind him.

"No!" she yelled. "You'll zap Poseidon, too!"

She held up a rock, squinting as she tried to aim it exactly.

"Don't knock him out!" Zeus warned.

"I won't," Hera promised. She sent the rock flying, and hit one of the birds. The bird lost its grip on Poseidon and tumbled toward the lake. Now there were three birds holding him.

Then an arrow went whizzing past Hera and

Zeus. It narrowly missed Poseidon and hit one of the three birds still holding him.

Hera spun around. "That was soo close!"

Apollo grinned. "Believe me when I tell you this—with my arrow I'll never miss."

Demeter was closest to Poseidon. Still wearing the helm, she tossed rocks at the remaining two birds, and Poseidon fell to the muddy ground with a thud.

"Oof! Thanks, guys!" he said, picking himself up.

Zap! Zeus blasted another line of birds out of the sky before they could reach Poseidon. Many of them were turning tail and squawking their way back to the forest in defeat. But there were still hundreds, maybe thousands more, all fixing their glowing red eyes on the Olympians.

"Get back into formation!" Zeus yelled.

 57

"Hestia, Poseidon, let's see if we can supercharge again."

Hestia and Poseidon raced toward Zeus, but before they could reach him, a boy their own age appeared at the edge of the marsh. He was holding a wicked-looking spear. And it was pointed right at Zeus.

CHAPTER SIX

The Boy with Red Eyes

S top!" yelled the new mystery boy. "Those are my birds!"

"Then tell them to back off!" Zeus cried as one of the Stymphalian birds swooped toward him. He quickly hurled Bolt. It slammed into the bird's metal body, causing it to spark and sizzle.

With a strangled cry the boy charged toward Zeus, crashed into him, and knocked him to the

ground. Then the boy poked Zeus's chest with the sharp end of his spear.

Realizing that the other Olympians were too busy fighting off birds to help him, Zeus shouted for Bolt. The magical weapon turned in midair, flew toward the boy, and zapped him in the shoulder.

"Yow!" The boy tumbled to the ground.

Zeus kicked the boy's sharp spear away and quickly jumped to his feet. Bolt hovered over the strange boy's chest, trapping him. There was no way he could move without getting zapped again.

Stepping closer, Zeus got a good look at his attacker for the first time. The boy's dark brown hair stuck up all over the top of his head, like spikes. Then Zeus noticed his eyes. The part that should have been brown or blue or green was red, and that part glowed just like the eyes of the Stymphalian birds!

"Let me up," the red-eyed boy demanded. "And stop attacking my birds!"

"Attacking? We're defending ourselves," Zeus protested, gesturing towards the other Olympians, who were still doing just that. "Those birds attacked us first."

"Only because you're trespassing!" the boy shot back. "They're just doing their job."

"By shooting us with metal arrows and raining down poisonous poop?" Zeus asked. "Nice."

The boy's eyes flared angrily. "Listen, if you don't—" He broke off and tried to sit up, but Bolt gave him a little jab, so he gave up and flattened onto the ground again.

"How about you call off your birds?" Zeus asked before the boy could speak again. "Then we can call a truce to talk about this."

The boy blinked his red eyes, but didn't

 63

answer. Instead, while still lying on his back, he put two fingers into his mouth and let out a loud, piercing whistle. At the sound the birds immediately stopped their attack.

They flew up above the lake, regrouping. Soon they began to zip in different directions, and Zeus realized that the birds were forming words again: "SO LONG, LOSERS!"

With squawks that almost sounded like laughter, they flew off over the forest.

The boy nodded at Bolt, his red eyes on Zeus. "Your turn. Can you call this thing off now?" he asked.

"Sure," Zeus said. "Come, Bolt!" The magic thunderbolt flew back to his hand and shrunk to the size of a dagger. Zeus tucked it into his belt as the boy jumped to his feet and picked up his spear.

The other Olympians rushed over to check

out the new boy. Hades helped Demeter along since her left ankle was obviously still bothering her. Apollo walked beside Hera, singing,

"The Stymphalian birds
were on the attack,
But the seven young heroes
did bravely fight back—"

He stopped midsong when he saw the boy up close, his blue eyes lighting up in surprise.

"Ares!" whooped Apollo. He raced to the boy and gave him a big hug.

The boy pushed him away and stepped back. "Huh?" He looked confused. "Do I know you?"

CHAPTER SEVEN

A New Olympian

D on't you remember me?" Apollo asked. "It *has* been a long time. That old Titan Iapetos captured you, me, and my sister, Artemis, when we were just little kids. Artemis and I finally escaped, but you didn't."

The others looked at Apollo in surprise.

"How come you never told us this story before?" Hera asked.

He shrugged. "You never asked."

Poseidon shook his head. "Dude, really? You spend two weeks on the road singing every song you can think up, but you couldn't tell us something so important?"

Apollo brightened. "Good idea! I should write a song about it."

"Is there anything else you haven't told us?" asked Hera.

"I don't think so," Apollo said, beginning to strum his lyre. "Now let me see." Then he started to sing, "The evil Titan Iapetos . . . What rhymes with Iapetos?"

"You don't know what you're talking about," Ares burst out. "Iapetos is my father!"

"If he told you he's your father, then he's a liar," Apollo said. He swept his hand toward the group. "You're an Olympian, just like all of *us*."

Ares's face turned bright red. His eyes

started to glow like they were on fire, and his hands clenched into fists. "You're the liar!" he yelled.

Zeus stepped between them. "You know, for a Titan you're kind of small," he pointed out to Ares. "Titans are giants, but you're more our size—Olympian-size."

"You look kind of like us too, even if you do have weird eyes," Poseidon added.

Zeus shot him a warning look. Something— maybe that spear—reminded him that this Ares was not somebody you wanted to get riled up unnecessarily. Especially since he had a bunch of attack birds under his control.

"I can prove my story," Apollo offered. "If I didn't know you when you were three, then I wouldn't know about that birthmark on your back. The one shaped like a dog."

The anger in Ares's face started to fade. "How

do you know about that?" He quickly looked over his shoulder, to make sure the mark wasn't showing.

"I told you, we grew up together," Apollo said. "A birthmark like that isn't easy to forget."

"It really looks like a dog?" Hera asked.

Ares ignored her. He leaned back against a tree, dazed. "I just don't know about this. . . . Why don't I remember you?"

"Maybe you'll remember this. I wrote my first song for us," Apollo told him. He began to sing in a sweet, magical voice. It sounded like tinkling bells and chirping sparrows and gave you goose bumps when you listened to it.

"Good night, good night, good night,
The stars are in the sky.
Good night, good night, good night,
The owls are going to fly—"

"That's a pretty lame song," Poseidon chimed in.

Apollo stopped singing. "Hey, I was only three."

Zeus looked over at Ares and saw that his red eyes were starting to fill with tears. Ares quickly brushed them away.

By now the other Olympians had gathered closer, curious and eager to hear Ares's story. The swampy air was damp and chilly around them, and Hestia gave a little shiver.

"I think . . . I remember," Ares said. "It makes sense. My Titan brothers—I wondered why they're all way bigger than I am. And Clymene—our mom—has nicknames for all of us. Prometheus is the Smart One, Epimetheus is the Silly One, Atlas is the Strong One, and Menoetius is the Vain One."

"And what about you?" Hera asked.

Ares frowned. "She always just calls me the Other One. And my brothers used to tell me that they found me in a cabbage patch when I was a baby, all curled up and no bigger than a slug."

"Aw, that's kind of cute," said Demeter.

"What about Iapetos?" Apollo asked.

"You know, he never has been very nice to me," Ares said carefully. "He always makes me clean out the in-between part of his toes."

"Ew!" shrieked Hera, looking grossed out.

"And when we get dinner, he never gives me any good parts of the chicken," Ares went on. "I get the beak and the feet. And he just laughs when my Titan brothers call me Slug. But if he ever hears me call Atlas 'Muscle Brain,' he makes me clean out the chicken coop all by myself."

"Because those so-called brothers of yours are big Titans, and you're just a puny human—at least in his eyes," Apollo said. "Don't you see?"

Ares nodded. "Yeah. I think I get it," he said, his voice flat.

Zeus stepped up to him. "This is so great, because we've been looking for you!" he said encouragingly.

"We didn't know it was *you*, specifically, but now we do," said Hera. "Pythia, the Oracle of Delphi, told us that we would find a new Olympian on this quest."

"You guys are on a quest?" Ares asked, looking interested.

"Well, right now we're just standing around talking," Poseidon joked lamely.

Zeus ignored his brother.

"King Cronus wants to destroy all the Olympians," Zeus told Ares. "But Pythia said we can fight back. We have to find magical objects to use against Cronus"—he patted Bolt—"and gather all the Olympians for the final battle against him and the other Titans."

Ares's red eyes flashed. "Battle? And I get to come with you?"

"For sure," Zeus answered.

As they talked, Hestia started a small fire using some dry leaves, and Hades grabbed some rocks to put around it. Demeter took some bread and cheese from her pack.

"Who's up for some grilled cheese?" she asked. The other Olympians all eagerly shouted, "Me!"

Whatever sad feelings Ares had had about finding out that Iapetos had kidnapped him vanished. "Battle! This is gonna be awesome!" he cried. He grabbed his spear in both hands and started moving around the marsh like he was fighting. "Take that! And that! Let's go!"

"Not so fast," Hera said. "Pythia sent us to find something else too—a magical object called an aegis. It's like a shield with golden tassels hanging from it. Do you know where it is?"

Ares shook his head. "No," he answered. "But it sounds kind of familiar. Like I might have seen it when I was younger. I have a dim memory of my brothers—I mean, those Titan guys who aren't my brothers—fighting over it once. But they fight over a lot of stuff."

"Maybe it's in your house?" Hestia suggested.

Ares nodded. "Yeah, we could go look."

"Is everybody forgetting something?" Poseidon asked. "Ares lives with six Titans. Not one, not two—six!"

"And they're probably wondering where I am right now," Ares said, looking up at the sky. Night was falling fast. "I've got to cook dinner."

"Maybe you can sneak around your house and look for it this evening," Hera suggested. "We could camp here tonight and wait for you to join us with the aegis in the morning."

Poseidon anxiously looked up at the sky. "I'm not staying here with those birds."

"Don't worry," Ares said. "I won't let them hurt you."

Poseidon's eyes narrowed. "Why do they listen to you, anyway?"

Ares shrugged. "I'm not sure. I used to escape to the swamp whenever I could when I was little. The birds always liked hanging around me. I started listening to their cries, and it was like I could understand them. I'm the only one who can command them."

"Kind of like how I can command Cerberus, my dog in the Underworld," Hades said. "Maybe it's part of your power as an Olympian."

Ares grinned. "Yeah, maybe," he said. "So we have a plan, right? I'll look for the aegis tonight, and tomorrow we'll go look for a battle!"

"Well, the first part of the plan sounds good," Zeus said. Then a thought struck him. "How do we know you're not going to bring the Titans back here?"

"Because I know I'm an Olympian now," Ares replied. "I wouldn't betray my real brothers and sisters. See you in the morning."

Zeus and the others watched the strange boy disappear into the darkness. Zeus was pretty sure that they were all thinking the same thing.

Would Ares really return to help them? Or would her bring the Titans—and trouble— back with him?

CHAPTER EIGHT

A Shattered Hope

Zeus had a troubled sleep that night—but the next morning Ares showed up bright and early. And alone, thankfully.

"So, what's our plan of attack?" Ares asked eagerly.

"Did you find the aegis?" Hera asked right away.

Ares shook his head. "My four brothers— I mean the four Titans—kept me busy doing stuff for them all night, like they usually do. The vain Menoetius dyed his hair blond and made me help style it. As if I didn't have enough chores. I barely had time to sleep."

Zeus was thoughtful. "We can't leave until we have the aegis. It's part of our quest! What if we got the Titans out of the house so we could search it?"

"You could trick them!" Hades chimed in. "Tell them there's some kind of emergency or something."

"They're always worried about the family sheep flock," Ares said. "I guess I could say the sheep got loose."

Hades pointed to his helmet. "Or I could conveniently *set* them loose."

Ares suddenly frowned. "Only, the Titans will make me go find the sheep with them."

"We'll search the house for the aegis while

you help round up the sheep," Hera suggested. "Then you can sneak away and meet us back here. We won't leave without you."

Ares looked pleased, even a little touched by what she said. "You mean it?"

"Of course!" Zeus answered. "No Olympians left behind."

"Thanks," said Ares, smiling for the first time.

"Well, what are we waiting for?" Hera asked. "Let's go get that aegis!"

Ares nodded. "Follow me."

When they stepped back onto the marsh, the Stymphalian birds didn't move a single metal feather. Ares led the Olympians around the lake. It was the blackest water Zeus had ever seen. Quiet and still, with flies and other water bugs hovering over its surface. A musty, moldy stench rose up from it.

"Sorry you had to grow up here, Ares," Apollo said, wrinkling his nose.

Ares shrugged. "It's not so bad."

Hades sniffed the air. "Smells pretty nice to me!" Hera rolled her eyes at that.

When they reached the opposite shore, it opened up to a big, green field surrounded by a fence.

"Epimetheus and Atlas are probably outside," Ares warned. "But they're lazy and are likely over by the fig trees, lounging around. We should be okay if we stick to the east side of the pasture."

The eight Olympians carefully made their way along the edge of the field, which was dotted with dozens of white sheep. Demeter was still limping, so Hades and Hestia lent her an arm to lean to keep her upright. Across the field they could see a Titan-size house. It was made of stone, with a roof of thatched straw. Smoke rose from its chimney.

Suddenly Ares let out a cry. "My ex-brothers are coming!" he hissed, squinting into the distance. "Everybody, get behind that boulder!" All seven Olympians quickly crouched down behind a boulder just a few yards in front of them.

Zeus turned to Hades. "Can you scout ahead for us?" he asked in a whisper. "And see where they go?"

Hades nodded, put on his Helm of Darkness, and disappeared just as the sound of voices reached them.

"I hate sheep," a Titan was saying in a whiny voice.

"That's Epimetheus," Ares whispered.

"I wish Father would let us fight for King Cronus," grumbled another, deeper voice.

"And that's Atlas," Ares added.

"The king's got soldiers all over the land," Atlas went on. "Word is, they're going to capture those annoying Olympians soon."

Epimetheus chuckled. "Ha! I bet Rhea will serve King Cronus up a tasty breakfast of them once they're caught."

At these words Zeus's blood went cold. He looked at his brother and sisters—Poseidon, Hera, Demeter, and Hestia—and they looked stunned too. "Rhea" was their mother's name!

It must be another Rhea, Zeus thought. *Our mother would never—*

"Serve her own children to the king, would she?" Atlas said. "Not even *our* mom would do that!" The Titans laughed.

Serve her own children to the king. Zeus looked into Hera's eyes. When she nodded sadly, he knew they were both thinking the same thing: that their mother was on the side of King Cronus!

Zeus felt his heart shatter into a million pieces. He had always dreamed that he would meet his mom one day. In his imagination she was sweet and kind. She would make him fig pudding, he'd thought, and tell him how proud she was of him for being the leader of the Olympians.

Now he was crushed, so crushed that he didn't even hear a loud bell ringing in the distance.

Ares nudged him. "That's the lunch bell. They'll be leaving the field now."

Once the coast was clear, none of the Olympians moved right away. Zeus figured his siblings, like him, were still thinking about what those Titans had said about their mother. Finally Hades returned and took off his helmet.

"They're in the house," he reported. Then he noticed the sad faces around him. "What's wrong?"

 85

"Well, it sounds like our mom, Rhea, is working with King Cronus," Poseidon explained. "Stinks, right?"

"I don't believe it," Hades said with a frown.

"But we heard one of the Titans say so," Demeter said sadly.

Hades shrugged. "What do Titans know? I just don't think our mother would do that."

"What our mother would or wouldn't do isn't something we have time to think about right now," Hera snapped. She turned to Zeus. "Come on. We have an aegis to find! You're supposed to be our leader, aren't you, Boltbrain? What's next?"

Zeus took a deep breath. Hera was right. They had a quest to finish.

"Hades, put your helm back on and open the gate to the pasture," Zeus commanded. "Ares, you go inside and tell all the Titans a thief has taken the sheep. When the house is empty, we'll go in."

"We shouldn't all go in," Apollo pointed out. "We should leave somebody outside to stand guard. To warn us if the Titans come back unexpectedly."

"I'll do it," said Demeter. "I wouldn't be much use hobbling around that big house anyway."

"I'll stand guard with you," Hestia offered, patting her sister's arm.

Hades nodded. "And after I open the gate, I'll come back and help the two of them keep a lookout," he said to Hestia and Demeter.

"Great," Zeus said. He pointed to Hera, Apollo, and Poseidon. "You guys come search the house with me. Ares, we'll meet you back at the edge of the forest afterward."

"And then we go find some monsters to battle, right?" Ares asked eagerly.

Zeus rolled his eyes. In his humble opinion this new brother of theirs was way too eager to fight. "Not unless we have to."

"All right. Here I go." Hades put on the helm and immediately disappeared. Leaving Hestia and Demeter behind, the rest of them moved as close to the house as they could. Hiding behind some thick bushes, they heard the sound of sheep bleating as the invisible Olympian herded them toward the open gate.

Then Ares took off for the house, running and yelling. "Mom! Dad! Somebody is stealing our sheep!"

CHAPTER NINE
Discovered!

Right away four giants lumbered out the front door of the big house. Peeking from behind the bushes, Zeus decided the Titans all looked kind of alike. Except one was taller than the others, another had enormous muscles, one was smaller and kind of chubby, and one had a big head of golden blond hair.

"Where's the thief?" the muscled one asked, and Zeus recognized Atlas's voice.

"He opened the gate and ran off into the trees," Ares lied. "I tried to chase him, but he was too fast."

"Well, thanks for nothing! You ruined our lunch!" whined the chubby one, who must have been Epimetheus, Zeus guessed from his earlier glimpse of him. The tall one was probably Prometheus.

"If we go chasing after him it'll make me sweat," said the blond one, flipping back his hair. Zeus figured he had to be the Vain One, Menoetius.

Now a fifth giant, taller and older than the others, stomped out of the house. His bushy brown beard was streaked with gray, and he wore a small hourglass around his neck, which hung from a leather cord. Iapetos, the father, obviously.

"What are you lunks doing, just standing

here?" he growled. "Let's get those sheep!"

The four Titan brothers thundered toward the pasture. As Ares started to follow them, a female Titan stepped out of the house. Her blond hair was piled up in fancy curls all over her head, and there was bright pink makeup on her cheeks that matched her pink lipstick. Dozens of bracelets dangled from her arms.

"Hey, Other One!" the accessorized Titan called out to Ares. "Stay here with me. I need help polishing my jewelry."

Iapetos grunted in Ares's direction. "You heard what your mother said. Go help her."

Ares nervously glanced toward where the heroes were hiding, and then ran back to the Olympian house.

"How are we supposed to search the house if it's not empty?" Hera whispered.

"It'll be okay," Zeus whispered back, hoping

he was right. "I'm sure Ares will distract his mom for us."

"Anyone want to borrow my helm?" Hades asked, suddenly appearing in front of them.

"I'll take it!" Hera said, snatching it from his hands. She slipped it on, becoming invisible. "Let's go!"

Hera, Zeus, Poseidon, and Apollo tiptoed up to the house. Zeus peeked through the crack between the open door and the door-jamb. He could hear Ares talking in a loud voice.

"So you want me to help you here in the kitchen, Mom?" he was asking. "The kitchen, on the left side of the house?"

"He's letting us know where he is, and that he's not alone," Hera hissed. "If we stay away from the kitchen, we'll be fine."

"Of course the kitchen, you idiot," they

heard Clymene, wife of Iapetos, say, clicking her tongue. "Honestly, Other One, you have even fewer brains than the Silly One!"

Zeus sneaked through the front door. He had been in a Titan's house before. Everything in it was much bigger than in a regular home, since the Titans were giants. The door opened up into a hallway. Against one wall was a wooden table twice as tall as Zeus, with a big pitcher on top. Farther along the hallway he could see doors leading to other rooms.

He turned back to the others. "Everybody pick a door and search the room beyond it," he said. "Just don't go into the kitchen."

Apollo and Poseidon nodded. Hera probably did too, but Zeus couldn't tell because she still wore Hades's helm. The other three Olympians quietly slipped into the house behind Zeus, and they all split up.

Zeus went into a door on the left. Just before he pushed through it, he glimpsed a door on the right push open and figured it was Hera, still invisible.

Meanwhile, Hera looked around inside the room she had entered. It was a pantry, with shelves holding big loaves of bread, dried meat, bowls of figs and olives, and baskets of carrots and onions. Dried herbs hung from the ceiling, filling the pantry with their scent.

Shiny. Metal. Tassels, Hera reminded herself. She looked around but didn't see anything fitting that description. So no aegis here. Then she heard Clymene again, this time very close by.

"Where are those rose petals?" the Titaness asked. "Other One, help me look for them in the pantry."

Yikes! Hera thought quickly. Even though she was invisible, she didn't want the Titaness bumping into her. She curled up in a corner of the room, under one of the shelves.

"I *must* wash my hair in rose petals tonight," Clymene was saying as she swept into the room wearing a bright pink robe. Hera saw Ares glance around nervously as he came in behind her. He was probably worried that one of the Olympians was hiding there. He was right!

"Everyone who matters will be at that temple," Clymene continued. "And when they hear me sing, well, I will surely get the fame that I deserve! My name will be known throughout the kingdom!"

She got a dreamy look on her face, but behind her Ares just rolled his eyes. Hera figured he must've heard Clymene brag like this before.

"And of course my beauty must match my

voice," she said. "Now then, Other One. Have you found the rose petals?"

Ares grabbed a clay jar off a shelf. "Right here."

"Excellent! While I prepare my bath, you may finish polishing my jewelry," she said. Ares sighed.

Hera let out a breath when he and Clymene and Ares left. She could hear the sound of Clymene's shiny bracelets jangling as she walked.

The bracelets . . . Hera suddenly had a thought. She raced out of the pantry and down the hallway, glancing in every room. She finally found what she was looking for—Clymene's bedroom, the last door on the right.

None of the others had reached it yet. She was sure it was Clymene's room, because the curtains were pink, and so was the cover on the bed. Tunics in glittery colors were messily scattered across the floor. Besides the bed, the biggest item in the room was a table pushed against the wall, with a chair in front of it.

Bracelets, flimsy scarves, and pots of makeup were scattered across the tabletop. Hera shinnied up the leg of a big chair to its seat, which was higher than her head, to get a better look.

And there it was, hanging from the wall. A bright, golden shield that could be slipped over your neck and worn to protect your chest and back. Gold tassels hung from its bottom.

Hera's hunch had been right. Someone who liked shiny things as much as Clymene did would love the aegis. It was way too small for a giant Titan. It looked like she had been using it as a mirror, though.

Hera reached up and took it off the wall, then stood there, trying to figure out how to get back down from the chair.

"My aegis! It's floating!" Clymene shrieked as Hera stood with it in her hands.

Hera groaned. She had forgotten that even though she was invisible, the aegis wasn't. Unless she was wearing it, that is. She quickly slipped it over her head, but it was too late. Clymene, in a pink robe, stormed out of the bathroom just as Zeus, Poseidon, and Apollo met up in the hallway. They'd been caught.

"Other One! What are these small people doing here?" she yelled. Her lips curled in disgust, like she was confronting vermin.

"Um . . . I don't know," Ares replied. "But I'll chase them out for you. Get out of here, you . . . small people!"

Zeus and the others broke into a run, heading back out the front door. Clymene watched them go, her mouth open in confusion and a look of horror on her face.

Once the Olympians were outside, Hera took off the helmet. "I did it!" she cried. "I found the aegis!"

Poseidon gave her a high five.

"Come on," Ares said urgently. "We've got to hurry away before—"

Bam!

A huge boulder landed in front of them, shaking the ground. Atlas came stomping toward them, his arm raised, ready to throw another huge rock. His brothers and father were behind him, holding enormous rocks too.

Iapetos pointed at Zeus and his companions. "Capture them. They're Olympians!" he yelled.

CHAPTER TEN

Missing

With a mighty heave Atlas pulled a small tree out by the roots and hurled it at the Olympians. Zeus reached for Bolt and flung it through the air. It grew as it flew, and sliced the tree trunk in half before it reached the Olympians. Then Bolt turned and flew back to Zeus's hand.

"Other One! Why aren't you beating up those guys?" Atlas yelled to Ares.

Ares stepped forward. "Because I'm an Olympian like them!" he said proudly. "And we're ready to do battle!"

His brothers started cracking up. "You? An Olympian? You're just a little slug!" Epimetheus crowed. "And you know nothing about battle."

Athena looked quizzically at Iapetos. "I thought Slug was our brother."

Iapetos shrugged. "Of course he isn't. Look at him! We're big! He's small! I captured him and we pretended he was family so he'd be our servant!" Scowling at Ares, he said, "This is your last stand, little Olympian!" With that, Iapetos removed the hourglass from around his neck.

"What's he doing?" Hera wondered aloud.

"He has power over time," Ares explained, sounding nervous. "The sand in that hourglass can stop time for whoever it touches. He'll freeze us and then take us to Cronus."

"You're smarter than we thought, Slug," Menoetius said. "But not smart enough to get away."

Grinning, Iapetos held up the vial of sand.

"Oh, no you don't!" yelled Poseidon. He jumped in front of Ares.

"So you like to control time? Well, it's bath *time*, Beardo!" he shouted. He pointed his trident at the bearded Iapetos. A blast of water hit the Titan's chest, but Iapetos barely noticed it.

"Bolt!" Zeus yelled. He pointed his thunderbolt at the hourglass, aiming a jagged charge of electricity at it. But Iapetos held up his palm, blocking and absorbing the charge.

Hera put Hades's helm back on, picked up broken pieces of boulder, and started hurling them at Iapetos and his sons. They only seemed to bother Epimetheus. "Ow! Ow! Who's doing that?" he wailed.

Clymene rushed out of the house in her pink bathrobe. "What is all this racket? I'm trying to take a bath!"

At the same time Apollo took out his bow and started shooting arrows at the Titans. However, they only brushed the arrows away with their big hands.

Iapetos laughed. "Foolish Olympians! Give up. Let us end this now." He held up the hourglass, tipping it toward them like he was going to douse them with sand.

Suddenly a loud whistle pierced the air. *Tweeeeeeeeeet!* It was Ares!

The Titans froze, anxiously looking up at the sky. It grew black overhead as the massive flock of Stymphalian birds raced to answer Ares's summons.

One of the birds swooped down, its red eyes blazing, and grabbed the vial from Iapetos's hands.

"Call off your pets, Slug!" Iapetos shouted, shaking his fist.

"No way!" Ares replied. And then to the Olympians he yelled, "Come on. Let's get out of here while the getting's good!"

The birds descended on the Titans as the Olympians raced away from the house. Metal feathers whizzed through the air, and globs of poisonous poop rained from the sky.

"Wait! Where are Hestia, Demeter, and Hades?" Hera shouted.

Zeus skidded to a stop. "They're standing guard." He quickly changed direction and headed toward the bushes, where they should have been hiding—only, they weren't.

"They're not here!" Zeus called to the others. "We can't leave them. No Olympian left behind!"

He felt an invisible arm grab him by the elbow. Then Hera took off the helmet and appeared in front of him. "They're probably in the forest, waiting for us," she said. "Come on!"

Zeus didn't argue. He hoped Hera was right. But in his heart he feared she might not be.

He, Hera, Poseidon, Apollo, and Ares all raced down the edge of the field, past the lake, and finally stopped at the edge of the forest.

"I don't see them anywhere," Zeus said. He circled around the marsh, staring down at the mud. "No footprints, either."

"Pythia will help us, have no fear. Let's just keep walking and wait until she appears," Apollo suggested.

"Hey, that's right," Poseidon said. "This *is* about the time Pythia usually shows up! We've got the aegis. We found the Olympian. That's when that misty stuff comes and Pythia appears."

"Right!" Zeus agreed. "So let's just walk and wait."

The Olympians walked and waited . . . and walked and waited . . . and walked and waited. Poseidon passed around some bread and cheese and apple-sized berries he had stolen from the Titan kitchen.

"There's no grilled cheese without Hestia," Poseidon said gloomily as they ate.

They walked and waited. The sun went down, and soon stars dotted the black sky. They stopped walking.

"I don't think Pythia's coming," Hera said finally.

"But she always comes," Poseidon protested.

"Listen, there's no point in waiting around here for that oracle forever," Ares said impatiently. "We need to keep going so we can battle King Cronus and his Cronies!"

"We can't do that until Pythia confirms that our current quest is finished and gives us a new quest," Zeus said stubbornly. "Besides, she might be the only one who can tell us how to find Hades, Hestia, and Demeter."

"But she hasn't shown up, has she?" said Hera. "So what do we do now, oh fearless leader of the Olympians?" she asked. There was more than a hint of sarcasm in her voice.

"If Pythia won't come to us, then we'll go to her," Zeus said. "We'll head for Delphi!"

Ares clapped him on the shoulder. "Great idea," he said. "And we can fight off the Cronies all the way there!"

Poseidon frowned at him. "That's not as much fun as it sounds."

"We need to head north, and then cross the sea to get to Delphi," Ares reported. "It's the fastest route."

"Chip will lead the way," Hera said. Still holding Hades's helm, she reached under the aegis for the amulet with her free hand, and dropped the helm in the process. "Okay, this is a little tricky," she said.

"Um, about that," Zeus said. "I'm thinking maybe we should pass the aegis around and see who it belongs to. . . ."

"What?" Hera asked, her blue eyes blazing. "But I found it!"

"Right, but usually when a magical object and its owner meet, something *magical* happens," Zeus pointed out. "And when the Titans were fighting us, the aegis didn't do anything."

Hera frowned. "Well, that was only one battle. Maybe its magic just hasn't kicked in for me yet."

"We need you to guide us with Chip," Zeus said, trying to reason with her. "And Hades entrusted you with his helm. With the aegis, that's three magical objects to juggle. Too many for one person."

"It's bad battle strategy," Ares agreed. "One soldier shouldn't hold all the weapons."

Hera sighed. "Fine," she said, slipping the aegis off. "It's kind of heavy anyway."

She handed it to Poseidon, who tried it on.

"Nothing," he said. Ares tried it on next, and then Apollo, and then Zeus.

As Zeus touched the aegis, he felt a little tingle in his fingertips. What could it mean? Was the aegis his? But he already had a magical object. Two if you counted Chip.

"I think Apollo should wear it for now," he said. "Because, Ares, at least you have your spear. And your birds."

Ares nodded. "The birds don't always come to me if I'm too far away from the swamp," he said. "But Apollo can have the aegis."

"Sounds fair to me," Hera agreed, and Poseidon nodded.

So Zeus handed the tasseled aegis back to Apollo, and then nodded at Ares. "Can you get us to the coast?" he asked him.

"Sure, follow me," Ares said. He made a fist and thrust it high in the air. "To battle!"

"I hope not," Hera mumbled.

They started to walk again, with Hera using Chip's glow and Zeus using Bolt's shine to light their path.

"Um, are we going to sleep tonight? Ever?" Poseidon asked after a while.

"Let's get out of this forest first," Zeus said. "Besides, we might spot Hades, Hestia, and Demeter. We've got to keep our eyes open."

After walking for another half hour, a strange sound interrupted the quiet night. *Thump-thump, thump-thump, thump-thump . . .*

"It's like drums beating," remarked Zeus.

They were nearing the edge of a cliff. Zeus got down on his knees and crawled to the brink of it to look over. The others followed him.

In the canyon below they saw thousands of Cronies—the half-giants that made up King Cronus's army. They stood in a circle around a huge bonfire. And next to the enormous blaze sat a giant, brass urn. The soldiers marched in formation around the fire and the urn, their heavy feet stomping on the canyon floor.

"What are they doing?" Poseidon asked out loud.

"They're marching around a giant urn, but what it contains, we may never learn," Apollo sang softly in rhyme-speak.

Ares jumped to his feet. "It's battle time!" he yelled. "Let's charge them!"

 112

"Ares, get down!" Hera hissed, pulling on his leg.

Down below, some of the marching Cronies stopped and gazed around. One of them pointed up at the Olympians.

"Look! More Olympians! Get them!"

"*More* Olympians?" Zeus exclaimed. "That must mean they have Hades, Demeter, and Hestia! We have to rescue them!"

A small group of Cronies scrambled up the rocky cliff side, headed right for them.

Zeus froze, suddenly unsure what to do. Things had never looked so bad. Three Olympians had been recaptured. Pythia seemed to have abandoned them. And the Cronies were hot on their heels.

"Come on, Bolt Breath!" Hera yelled at him. "You know what we have to do!"

"Put our magical objects together?" Zeus asked.

"No time. Let's run!" Hera yelled.

Zeus didn't argue. He and the others turned and raced into the darkness with the Cronies pounding after them. *Just another typical day for the Olympian heroes in training,* thought Zeus.

He picked up his pace, determined to find Pythia. Because he had a hunch that wherever the oracle was, she needed rescuing too!